Kathleen Pennell

CIRCUS OF FEAR

by Kathleen Pennell

illustrated by
Lauren Pennell

CIRCUS OF FEAR
PONY INVESTIGATORS #3

Library of Congress Number: 2002102178
International Standard Book Number: 1-930353-34-0

Printed 2002 by
Masthof Press
219 Mill Road
Morgantown, PA 19543-9516

Dedicated

to

Karen and Gary, John and Sue
Beth and Dennis, Melissa and Gary

Special thanks to:

Miss Paige Landau
Lancaster Country Day School student

Miss Emely Perez
Lancaster Country Day School student

Contents

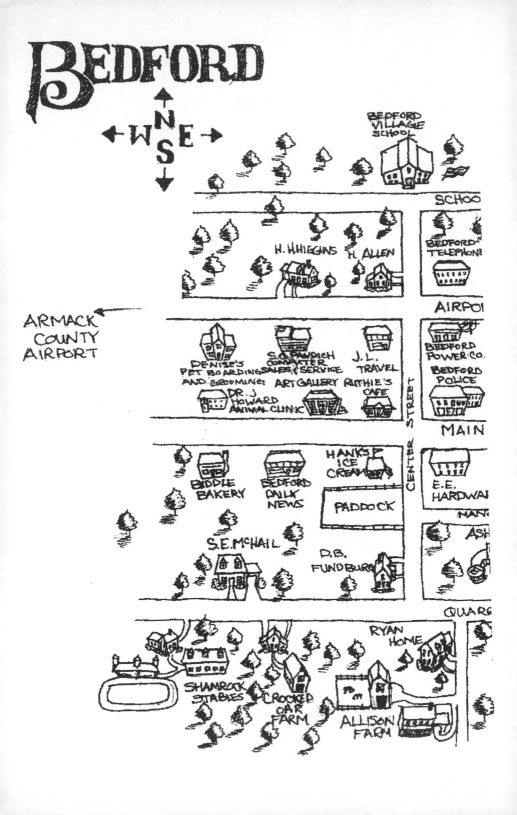

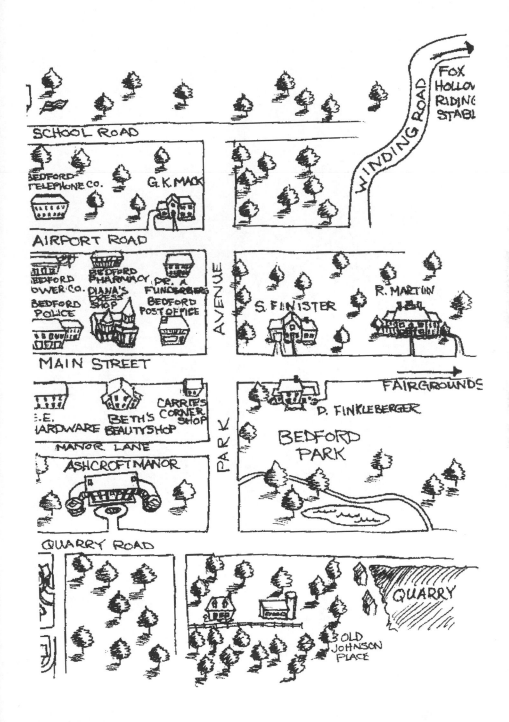

CHAPTER 1

Revenge Takes Careful Planning

The lion paced back and forth in his cage. He butted the door with his head. The metal catch rattled against the lock then settled back into place. Growling softly, he switched his tail in irritation and ambled to the other end of cage. He turned in a circle twice before settling his muscled body on the floor.

The clown stepped into the shadow of a nearby tent. All was hidden except for the huge circles of white outlining the eyes. The feline giant slowly turned his majestic head. The approach of the clown was mirrored in the reflection of his golden eyes. It was the same clown from the previous night. Only tonight the clown made sure where the lion trainer was before setting out. Revenge takes careful planning.

The clown drew surgical gloves over each hand. The hands stretched inside the gloves. It was a good fit. From the folds of the polka-dotted suit the hands drew out a short, rectangular object. The thumb of the left hand flicked a switch and the blade flipped out of its hiding place. The glint of the blade shone in the half

1

moon. The gloved hand reached inside the other pocket and pulled out a chunk of raw meat encased in a plastic bag. The meat was freed from the bag and placed on the edge of the cage. The hand clutched the knife; then it cut a one-inch slit into the fleshy part of the dripping mass. Placing the knife beside the slab of meat, the hand felt for the dark medicine bottle in a concealed pocket. The lid was popped off and the bottle tipped over. A white pill fell into the gloved hand then was carefully pressed into the slit.

The lion ran his large, rough tongue around his mouth. Saliva dripped in a puddle between his paws. Cautiously, the lion rose to his feet. Eyeing the clown suspiciously, he moved toward the bars that separated him from what he wanted.

The lion lowered his head as the hand slowly slid the meat between the bars. For a second, the lion studied the clown's face; then he reached forward and sank his teeth into the raw mass and retreated to the far side of the cage. There, the lion sat down with the meat between his paws. He ripped apart a large chunk. Chewing slowly, he stared unblinkingly at the clown. The pill was swallowed unnoticed.

The clown slipped back into the shadow of the tent. Now, the waiting began . . . five, ten, fifteen minutes. The massive beast yawned, rolled over on his side, and fell asleep.

The dark figure left the cover of the tent and stepped to the front of the cage. After a careful check over each shoulder, the clown drew the bolt back from its catch and steadied the door so that it remained closed. The lion would sleep for at least three hours. There was plenty of time for the clown to get away. Plenty of time to establish an alibi. Everyone would have to account for

his whereabouts on the night the lion es-
caped. Smiling with satisfaction, the
clown returned to the cover of the shadow.

*   *   *   *

Sam Landau mopped his damp face with a red
handkerchief and replaced his dusty hat with a practiced
sweep of his hand. "That'll be thirty dollars even," he
said as he handed them a bill for the feed.

His daughter, Paige, hopped down from the truck.
Amy Jo Ryan and Becky Allison were too busy worrying
about the size of the bill to pay her any mind.

Amy Jo gulped as quietly as she could. Grabbing
Becky by the arm, she smiled at Sam, nodded at Paige,
and steered her friend into the stable. "How much have you
got?" she asked. Dollar bills spilled out as she snagged a
fistful of coins from the bottom of her jeans pocket.

Becky looked doubtfully at the dollar bills float-
ing to the stable floor. She opened her billfold. Inside
were bills neatly arranged in ones and fives. Walking over
to the tack trunk, she counted out eighteen dollars and
seventy-five cents in change. "Well, there it is," she said.
"I hope you have the rest."

Amy Jo scooped up the crumpled bills from the
stable floor and tossed them beside Becky's pile. She
muttered as she counted then recounted the amount.
"Looks like we have enough with about five dollars to
spare," she said with a sigh. "Only enough left over for
some ice cream cones and then we're tapped out."

The girls turned as they heard the sound of footsteps at the entrance to the barn. Paige's two dark

pigtails flopped from side to side as she looked back and forth on her way down the aisle. "I've never been in here before," she began wistfully. "It's really nice. I sure wish I could have a pony. Do you think I could keep a pony here if I save enough money to buy one?"

Amy Jo sighed as Paige walked up to her. "Now, Paige, we've been through this a hundred times before at school."

Paige's huge blue eyes looked as unhappy as they always did whenever they had this conversation. "I know, but now I have a job and I'm going to save a lot of money over the next few weeks."

Amy Jo looked astounded. Paige was just as tall as the other two girls, but she was a full two years younger. "A job?!" Now Amy Jo was peeved. "Doing what?" she asked, glaring at her from head to foot.

Paige, seeing that she had the advantage, strutted airily down the aisle toward Ginger's stall. She reached in and stroked the pony's muzzle and made cooing sounds, stretching the misery as long as possible. Ginger Snap nodded her head. Where's my treat, she seemed to ask.

"Hank set up an ice cream stand at the circus and I was the first one to ask if I could work for him," said Paige, a note of victory in her voice. "He says he doesn't think he can manage without me," she said, stretching the truth just a little bit.

Now, it was Becky's turn to look surprised. "Hank gave you a job?"

"Sure," said Paige as she trailed along to Oreo's stall. The mare was black in the front and back with a white stripe around her middle. Oreo Cookie looked doubtfully at the stranger but allowed herself to be stroked. The mare lifted her muzzle so that the girl could scratch her under the chin.

"You're only nine years old and  Hank gave you a job just like that?" said Amy Jo, snapping her fingers for effect.

"Well," Paige hedged, "not exactly just like that." Her shoulders sank ever so slightly as she edged closer to Oreo's stall.

Oreo stepped forward and lowered her head. She liked to be scratched between her ears, too.

Suspicion set in as Amy Jo slowly crossed her arms and cocked her head. "Okay, Paige, out with it," she said, her patience wearing thin. "How'd you bully Hank into giving you this job?"

"Well!" Paige sputtered, feeling somewhere between offended and found out. Finally, she decided to confess the whole thing, but only because she figured Amy Jo would get the truth out of Hank anyway. She always did. "I mean," she started again, more softly, "as soon as I found out he was setting up a stand at the circus, I went into the ice cream store and asked him for a job, that's all."

Amy Jo tapped her foot on the stable floor, arms still crossed. "And . . ." she prodded.

Paige knew when she had been beaten. "Okay, okay, I went in every day for a week and . . . well, more or less, begged."

Amy Jo and Becky exchanged knowing looks. Becky gave Paige good marks for going after what she really wanted. Amy Jo was foot-stomping, green-eyed jealous.

"I admire you for getting a job," said Becky as she turned back to the tack trunk where the girls had laid their money.

"Yeah, we just wish we'd gotten there first," muttered Amy Jo.

Suddenly, Paige felt enormous relief that she'd found out about the ice cream stand before they did. But, to play it safe, she decided to change the subject fast. "Dad and I were at the circus earlier delivering hay and feed to the carnival horses. Look what I picked up," she said, digging a folded piece of paper out of her back pocket. She stepped between the older girls and opened it up.

A man with black eyes and dark, slicked-back hair was standing back to back with a beautiful woman. Her eyes were an unnatural shade of green, almost emerald. Her light hair was shoulder length and wavy. She wore a floor-length, sequined dress. The man held a knife in his right hand. It was polished silver; the same color as the woman's dress. Neither of them smiled.

"It looks sort of creepy," said Becky, goose bumps springing to the surface of her skin.

Amy Jo took the paper and studied it for a few seconds. "Wouldn't want to meet him in a dark alley," she decided, returning it to Paige.

"I wouldn't be too crazy about meeting her either," admitted Becky. She turned back to the tack box and double checked the amount of money they had. She carefully separated the bills from the coins and followed the other two girls out of the barn where Paige's father was patiently waiting.

"Here you are," said Becky as she handed the money to Mr. Landau. "Thanks for bringing the feed on such short notice."

"Yeah, thanks," echoed Amy Jo half-heartedly, patting her flat jeans pocket.

Sam gave a small salute with his hand before turning on the ignition. He twisted his neck around and carefully backed up the truck. Paige threw her arm out the side window, waving wildly while Sam drove the truck towards Quarry Road.

The girls stared at the tail lights of the retreating feed truck until it passed Amy Jo's house halfway down the lane. A few coins jingled in their pockets as they walked back to the barn. Sacks of horse feed were piled in the middle of the stable floor.

Amy Jo pushed her wispy bangs aside. "You grab this end with me and we'll drag it into the feed stall," she said, pulling the first bag upright. "Otherwise we'll have to ask your dad to help us when he gets home from work."

Becky nodded as she took her place beside her friend. "He'd do it, but he's tired after working at the bank all day."

"My dad used to help me stack the ponies' feed before he died." Amy Jo could finally talk about him without instant tears coming to her eyes. "He'd get home from the police station in the city and follow me right up here to watch me ride."

After the last bag had been leaned against the wall in the feed stall, the girls wiped the dust from their hands and stepped into their ponies' stalls.

Ginger nudged Amy Jo's arm. "Okay, okay, Ginger, just give me a minute," Amy Jo said affectionately as she reached into her pocket. She stuck her face between the slats that separated Oreo and Ginger's stalls. "I think it was a mistake buying these ponies Starbursts," she complained.

"I know," Becky nodded. "Oreo kicks the stall door every time she hears me crunching the candy wrapper." Deep in thought, Becky continued to stroke her pony's back.

Oreo dipped her head down and nosed around the stall floor for any remnants of hay. "How much hay do we have left?" Becky asked.

Amy Jo thought for a second while she cleaned the soggy hay out of Ginger's water bucket. "Four bales, maybe," she answered. "Sam delivers hay, too. That's our next phone call. There's only one problem."

"What's that?" asked Becky as she pulled straw from Oreo's tail.

"We only have five dollars left, remember?"

"Oh, yeah," muttered Becky.

Amy Jo tossed the green-colored water through the open paddock door. "We wouldn't need as much hay if Ginger didn't put half of it in her water bucket," she said disgustedly, placing the bucket on its hook and re-filling it with clean water.

Ginger swished the fresh water with her nose, splashing part of it on the stall floor. Then she drank deeply of the cool water. Amy Jo kissed her pony on the neck and ran her hand over the mare's back.

After giving their ponies a final pat, the girls secured the stall doors and flung themselves side by side on top of the tack trunk. They leaned their heads back against the wall and kicked the side of the trunk. They took turns saying, "Hm," as money-making ideas surfaced and sunk in their minds.

Amy Jo bolted upright. "I've got an idea!"

Becky looked over with guarded enthusiasm. Amy Jo's ideas had gotten them into a lot of trouble in the two months since the Allisons had moved to Bedford. "What?"

"The circus is in town, right?" Amy Jo asked.

"Right."

Amy Jo leaned towards Becky.
"Well, don't kids just love to take pony
rides at the circus?"

"Sure," Becky answered, trying to rein in her
enthusiasm.

"How about if we take the ponies to the carnival
and ask for a job giving pony rides?!" Amy Jo jumped
off the tack box, grabbed the saddle soap, and began
cleaning her tack.

Becky sat up and watched her friend furiously
scrubbing away at her saddle. It was so unlike Amy Jo to
come up with a harmless idea, she hardly knew how to
react. "That's not a bad idea," she was forced to admit.

Amy Jo looked up from buffing the leather on the
saddle skirt. "What do you mean 'that's not a bad idea'?
It's a great idea! We're going to make lots of money."
Amy Jo thought for a second. "Wait'll ole Paige hears
about this," she muttered under her breath. "And we'd
better make it in the next two weeks," she said turning
back to her friend, "'cause that's when we're going to
run out of hay." Amy Jo threw a sponge to Becky. "Come
on, grab your saddle and get to work."

Ever practical Becky thought of their next step.
"There's probably a manager or someone we need to ask,"
she said as she hopped down from the tack trunk. "We'll
have to take halters and lead ropes along so we can tie
the ponies somewhere while we're in the office."

Amy Jo nodded her approval. "Don't want the bit
hurting their mouths while they're tied up. If we hurry, we
can catch someone before the evening crowd gets there."

"Yeah, before it gets dark in case that man with
the knife is around," said Becky, suddenly shivering.

9

CHAPTER 2

A Sticky Wicket

As the girls tied their ponies to a hitching post beside the main office, angry voices raged from within the double-wide trailer. They opened the screen door but hesitated before stepping through. A dark-haired man was seated at a desk calmly working on some papers while a war was being waged behind a door marked "Manager's Office."

"I had nothing to do with it!" a voice shouted from the inner office.

"It's your responsibility to see that the cage door is locked before you leave for the night!" returned another voice, equally angry.

"I did!"

"You couldn't have! And if it happens again, you're fired!"

There was silence for a few seconds. Then, heavy footsteps rushed to the door and tore it open. A man flushed with anger turned back for a second and faced the manager. "That cage was locked when I left!" he declared. He slammed the manager's door and huffed and fumed his way towards the exit.

The girls pressed themselves against the door before the man ran over them in his haste to leave.

*　　*　　*　　*

The carnival manager studied the girls for a few moments through rimless glasses. "You girls sure you're eleven?" asked Mr. Barney. "You look kind of small."

Amy Jo straightened her back and raised her chin. "Well, we're eleven all right," she said a bit saucily.

"What she means is," Becky covered quickly, "we're not very tall for our age, but we're very responsible."

Mr. Barney pulled the collar away from his ample neck. *An escaping lion and a huffy eleven-year-old*, he thought to himself. *I don't need this today.* "We've never had pony rides at this circus before," he said, glancing at his watch.

Looking at his watch was a bad sign. Amy Jo decided she'd better do some fast talking if they expected to get this job. "You know tons of kids are gonna swarm all over this place just to ride our ponies. I mean, we're pretty famous around here," she began with wide sweeps of her arms. "And after that they'll buy ice cream, ride the Ferris wheel, and pour into the big top just spending zillions of dollars on cotton candy and popcorn." Out of the corner of her eye she saw that the manager was sitting up. *At least he's paying attention.* "Why you'll have to institute crowd control just to keep the hordes of people in line." Another quick peek told her that he was almost there. "You'll wonder how you made any money at all before we got here," she finished breathlessly.

Mr. Barney leaned back in his chair and rubbed his chin. "Well, we could give it a try," he stated vaguely.

Amy Jo thought desperately. "We'll give you a cut of the money we take in!"

Becky's mouth dropped open.

He tapped his finger tips on his desk a few times then looked up sharply. "You give me twenty-five cents for every dollar you take in and it's a deal."

Amy Jo's eyes bulged, but Becky stepped
in before her friend could complain. "We'll take
it!" she quickly agreed. "May we start tonight?"

Mr. Barney carefully smoothed down the few hairs
on the top of his head, wondering how he'd let this freckle-
faced kid talk him into such a hair-brained scheme. "Okay,"
he said rather sourly. His face brightened as he asked, "Your
ponies don't buck or kick or anything, do they?"

"Oreo and Ginger buck and kick?" said Amy Jo in
good humor. She had decided that seventy-five cents on the
dollar was better than nothing.

Mr. Barney slumped just a bit then perked up.
"Bite?" he added hopefully.

"Never!" Becky assured him.

"Oh, well, gave my word, can't very well go back
on it now . . . can I," he stated, but there was a hint of a
question as he looked at the girls. Amy Jo folded her arms
and shook her head, but not saucily this time. There's
nothing worse than a smart aleck winner and she knew the
power of winning gracefully.

Mr. Barney sighed. "Oh, well, there you have it then.
A deal's a deal. Give your names to my assistant, Karl
Ferrell, on your way out," he had already returned to his
work. "He's got a map of the grounds and can show you
where the small practice ring is. You can use that."

"Thanks, Mr. Barney," said Amy Jo, as they turned
to leave. "You won't be sorry."

"I hope not," he answered, giving them a grimace
which they interpreted as a smile.

Mr. Ferrell stopped writing and looked up as the
girls walked through the door that separated Mr. Barney's
office from his. He carefully placed his pen in a holder to

13

the left of his desk and leaned his thin frame back in his chair. "What can I do for you?" he asked quietly. His pale eyes looked at one then shifted to the other.

"My name's Amy Jo Ryan and this is Becky Allison." Amy Jo nodded in her friend's direction. "Mr. Barney said we could start giving pony rides tonight."

"He told us you have a map so we can see where the practice ring is," Becky added.

Mr. Ferrell stared at them for a few seconds then at the intercom.

Amy Jo gave Becky a side glance which said, *He's going to press the button on that intercom and try to talk Mr. Barney out of it!*

"All right," he finally said. Mr. Ferrell reached in a drawer and drew out a map. With long, slender fingers he flattened the corners of the map on top of his desk. His eyes wandered over it for a moment, then he carefully circled a spot. "It's here, next to an abandoned trailer. Nobody lives there so you won't be in anybody's way," he said, looking up to make sure they were watching. "Just turn right when you leave here and go past the big top. It's right after that."

"Right," Amy Jo nodded her head as she picked up the map Mr. Ferrell had refolded.

"Thanks," said Becky, following Amy Jo through the screen door.

Oreo and Ginger had been tied where they could graze the half hour they waited for the girls to return. They'd spent the time swatting flies with their tails and occasionally touching noses. When the screen door opened, they neighed softly as the girls popped through and trotted down the steps.

Amy Jo stroked Ginger's neck and unwrapped a piece of Starburst candy. It was her way of saying thank you for

being good. The mare crunched the candy between her back teeth then licked Amy Jo's hand.

"That was a close call back there,"
commented Amy Jo. "When the manager said they'd
never had pony rides before, I didn't think he'd let us do it."
She gave Ginger a quick kiss on the nose before unlatching
the halter and placing it in her saddlebag.

Becky tossed the empty candy wrapper into a trash
bin then tightened Oreo's girth. She slipped her foot in the
stirrup and swung her right leg over the saddle. "I'll tell you
something, Amy Jo. When you start talking, you can get
people to agree to just about anything."

Amy Jo opened her mouth to say thanks, then she
closed it. She wasn't so sure it was meant as a compliment.

They rode a few steps in silence. "Did you catch
Mr. Ferrell, when we asked for a map?" Amy Jo asked.
"I got the feeling he was going to call Mr. Barney to tell
him we'd be in the way or something."

Becky nodded. "I noticed, but at least he didn't and
we got the job. After we check out the riding ring, why don't
we go to my house and make up a bunch of signs. What do
you think we ought to charge?"

Amy Jo drew her eyebrows together and thought.
"Well, how about five dollars a ride?"

Becky turned in her saddle. "Five dollars a ride!? Nobody's going to pay five dollars a ride. How about one dollar?"

Amy Jo sighed a few times. "Oh, all right," she
agreed, pulling up in front of the sign at the big top. "Hey,
what's this?"

Becky reined in Oreo beside Ginger and read out
loud, "'Zorbon the Great and his beautiful assistant, Zelda,
performing nightly in the big top.'"

Amy Jo leaned forward in her saddle and studied the picture. Zorbon's black, piercing eyes stared back at them from the poster. He had his arms crossed at his chest and in both hands held a long knife.

Zelda stood at an angle, her left hand on her hip. She was nearly as tall as Zorbon in her three-inch heels.

"It's the same two people Paige showed us this morning," Becky remarked.

Amy Jo nodded. "He must be some kind of knife thrower," she decided, settling back in her saddle.

"And Zelda is the lovely lady he throws the knives at." Becky shuddered. "Don't think I'd want to be Zelda just in case he missed."

"Well, it's a sticky wicket if you ask me," Amy Jo commented as she turned Ginger away from the tent.

Oreo trotted to catch up with her buddy. Becky reined in and settled back in the saddle. "What's a sticky wicket?"

Amy Jo tilted her head in thought for a moment. "It's like when the bad guys are chasing Sherlock Holmes and Dr. Watson and they try to run out the back door, but it's locked. So they quickly find another way to escape."

"I get it," said Becky thoughtfully. "A sticky wicket is a bad situation to be in, right?"

"Right," answered Amy Jo.

The riding ring was about two hundred feet from the Big Tent. Next to it, standing all alone, was a small trailer. One side had a slightly caved-in look as if something had run into it. Its only neighbors were the riding ring and three paddocks for the circus horses.

Becky looked over the riding ring. Amy Jo studied the trailer.

"Strange it's out here all by itself," mused Amy Jo.

"I think it's great that nobody's  nearby," Becky began hopefully. "It's more room for us when all our customers show up."

"No," said the young detective, gesturing beyond the ring. "I'm talking about the trailer."

Becky turned her gaze in that direction. "They probably just dumped it back there to get it out of the way. Anyway, he said it was abandoned, so nobody lives there."

"That's odd," Amy Jo remarked.

"What's odd?"

Amy Jo nodded to the trailer. "It has curtains at the window and steps leading to the door. Why would it have curtains and steps if it's been abandoned?"

Becky shrugged her shoulders in total disinterest. "Let's ride back," she said, turning Oreo's head towards home. "We need to make some signs."

Amy Jo lingered for a few more seconds as she eyed the trailer. Then she turned and squeezed Ginger's sides, asking the mare to pick up a trot.

As Ginger reached Oreo's side, the mares realized that they were heading back home. They snorted and side-stepped, eager to slip into a canter and return to their stalls where hay, water, and a good brushing awaited them.

Amy Jo eased back on her reins to keep Ginger in check. "You're right, Beck. We've got to get those signs made so that those 'tons of kids' I talked about can find their way to the ring."

Becky laughed. "My mom always says to be careful what you wish for."

"Yeah, you've got to be careful, all right," Amy Jo said under her breath as she took one last look over her shoulder at the trailer.

CHAPTER 3

A Wild Goose Chase

It was steamy. The sun slipping below the horizon hadn't dropped the temperature a bit. Dusk was upon them and there were still "a ton of kids swarming" outside the ring. And all of them were whining.

Ginger's head hung low. Occasionally, she looked up to glare at the crowd of kids outside the ring. Her coat, usually chestnut, was sandy now from the dirt and grime mixed in with sweat.

Oreo needed a bath. Normally, she was black and white, but at the present she looked like a four-legged brownie. She snorted and pawed every time she stopped, which wasn't often enough for her liking.

Amy Jo's shoulders sagged as she dragged Ginger along.

"We should have made up one more sign this afternoon, Beck," she said.

Becky looked up. She needed a bath, too. "What do you mean?"

"The one that says 'temporarily out of order,'" Amy Jo replied.

Becky dredged up half a smile as she pictured an 'out of order' sign hanging around each pony's neck. Her dark hair and pale face were covered with a thin film of

19

dust. "Well, there are only four more kids waiting over there now," she said, hoping no one would show up at the last minute. "Then we're done."

A faded smile and a slurred thank you was all they could muster as the last customer left the ring. They walked their ponies out of the ring towards the edge of the paddock. After untacking the mares, they grabbed two hoses lying coiled on the ground.

Amy Jo tightened her grip on Ginger's lead rope as she turned on the faucet. "Now, steel yourself, girl," she said, knowing they were in for a fight.

Placing her thumb over the nozzle, Amy Jo sprayed water over the mare's back. Ginger danced around trying to escape. "I hate to do this to you, girl," said Amy Jo sadly as she aimed the hose at Ginger's dirt-caked face. The mare lifted her head and stepped backwards.

By contrast, Oreo stood calmly while Becky rubbed the dirt off the white part of her mare with the force of the water.

Amy Jo looked at her friend in disgust mixed with envy. Becky had tossed the end of the lead rope over the mare's neck. While Amy Jo was playing "Ring Around the Rosy" with Ginger, Oreo was steady as a rock while the water dripped down her sides.

After grazing the mares for a few minutes, they opened the gate to an empty paddock and turned the ponies loose. The carnival horses in the adjoining paddock lifted their heads, stared for a moment, then went back to grazing.

The girls pulled dollar bills and coins out of their pockets and sank to the ground. The ponies lifted their heads over the top of the fence and watched them count.

"Eighty-four dollars," sighed Becky.
Amy Jo flopped back on her
elbows. "Seems like it should be about
five thousand," she moaned. Ginger snorted in agreement.

From the other side of the fence, they heard the
door of the trailer shut. The girls jumped up and turned
around. Lights had been turned on. They saw the
outline of a woman through the window. Her hands
slid slowly up to her hips. She stood motionless staring
in their direction. Stepping back, she raised her arm and
drew the curtains shut, blocking their view.

Becky frowned. "What was that all about?"

"And Mr. Ferrell said nobody lives there,"
sneered Amy Jo, craning her neck to get a better look.
"I just knew there was something mysterious about
that trailer. We're looking at trouble, that's for sure."

Becky lifted her eyebrows. "Mysterious? Trouble?
Why do you always have to make such a big deal out of
everything?" she asked as she turned away. "Maybe she
just moved in and nobody told him about it. Come on.
If we hurry, we might be able to ride the Ferris wheel
before it closes."

"Well, *you* never suspect *anybody*!" Amy Jo shot
back. "There are a lot of sneaky people running around,"
she continued. "You just aren't looking for them." Amy
Jo stood for another moment staring at the trailer, then
she raced to catch up to her friend. "I wonder who she
is," she muttered under her breath.

*   *   *   *

"Cuttin' it pretty fine," the ticket taker said, looking at his watch.

"When do you close?" asked Amy Jo, giving her ticket to the Ferris wheel operator. His name tag said "Ernie."

"Ten minutes," Ernie said.

"Good thing we hurried," said Amy Jo as she hurried to the seat.

"Yep," said Ernie.

"Better late than never," quipped Becky.

"Yep," repeated Ernie.

"Looks like we have the whole Ferris wheel to ourselves," Amy Jo noted, as Ernie secured the bar across their seat.

"Yep," he said again.

"A man of few words," Becky mumbled as they rose into the air.

"Yep," Amy Jo chuckled.

The breeze felt good. Amy Jo lifted her damp auburn hair, allowing the air to cool the back of her neck.

They breathed deeply and closed their eyes, enjoying the rhythm of the Ferris wheel. Effortlessly it glided to the bottom past the ticket stand then up again to the top. Forgotten were the annoying cares of the day. They sunk low and rested their heads on the back of the seat.

Suddenly, the wind picked up. They opened their eyes and sat up. Dark clouds had formed against the horizon. And the dark mass was headed in their direction!

The Ferris wheel made another revolution . . . all the way down and back up to the top. Then everything stopped. And the lights went off.

The girls leaned over the side and looked down. Nobody was there. Clouds that had seemed far away a few moments ago were overhead now. What had been a  refreshing breeze was now a strong gust of wind, making the empty seats creak as they rocked back and forth.

Becky groped for Amy Jo's arm. "I want to get off!" Her voice was filled with panic.

"Good idea," answered Amy Jo, struggling to make sense of what was happening. "Right now might not be the best time though." She leaned over to look down, but their seat tilted forward and began to rock. "Whoa!" she said shakily.

"Don't do that!" Becky's hands gripped the bar.

"Hey, Ernie!" Amy Jo shouted. "Why'd you stop the Ferris wheel?"

No answer.

"Is anybody down there?" Becky's voice seemed to echo in the growing darkness.

From a distance, they saw people leaving the big top and heading for their cars.

Amy Jo cupped her hands around her mouth. "Hey! Can anybody hear us down there?!"

"He couldn't have just left, could he?" asked Becky, looking anxiously around.

"No, he's just playing a nasty trick on us," Amy Jo answered. Then she muttered under her breath, "I hope." She leaned as far forward as she could without rocking the seat, but all she saw was a network of criss-crossing metal.

"What are we going to do?" Becky strained to look over the side without making the seat move.

23

"Maybe we could take turns calling for help," Amy Jo suggested. "Somebody's bound to hear us . . . eventually."

"All right," Becky agreed. "You go first."

Amy Jo took a deep breath and cupped her hands around her mouth. "Help! Somebody! We're up here in the Ferris wheel!"

A fork of lightning reflected in the hazel flecks of Becky's eyes. "This isn't a very good time to get stuck up here," she worried.

"I know," Amy Jo agreed, feeling the first drops of rain on her face. "We've got to get off this thing before that storm hits."

Suddenly, the lights came back on. The girls blinked and the next moment, the Ferris wheel jolted to a start. It took forever, but finally their seat was at ground level. And there was Ernie.

"What's the big idea stopping the Ferris wheel at the top like that?!" Amy Jo demanded angrily, as he released the bar.

"I'm awful sorry, girls." Ernie nervously dragged his fingers through his graying hair, revealing his deep widow's peak. "Andy walked up and said the manager wanted to see me. Said he'd watch the ride for me. But when I got to Mr. Barney's office, he wasn't there."

"Who's Andy?" demanded Amy Jo.

"Andy's one of the clowns." Ernie frowned, drawing in his thin lips. "At least I thought it was Andy. His voice was a little hoarse, but he had on Andy's clown suit." He thought for a second. "Come to think of it, the clown wasn't quite as tall as Andy either."

"Why would he leave us like that?"
Becky frowned.

"That's the problem," he said nodding in the direction of the trailers. "I saw Andy on the way back and asked him why he sent me on a wild goose chase. He didn't know what I was talking about."

Ernie stuck his bony hands in his pockets and looked at the ground. "Fact is, there's been so much trouble going on around here lately, I could lose my job over this." His pale eyes studied the girls. "If the boss ever finds out about it."

"We wouldn't want you to lose your job, Ernie," Becky mellowed, casting a quick glance at Amy Jo.

Amy Jo studied him for a moment. "What do you mean there's been so much trouble around here lately?"

Ernie looked over his shoulder. "I shouldn't really be talking about it."

Amy Jo leaned forward, curiosity replacing her anger. "Maybe we can help."

"I don't see how you can help, but it looks like I owe you one." Ernie sighed and shook his head. "A week ago," Ernie began, stealing another glance over his shoulder. "somebody messed with the safety net for the high wire act. Of course, the Bendinis always check it just before climbing the ladder, so they fixed it right away. Show went on like nothing happened."

The girls exchanged speechless glances.
"Then," Ernie's eyes swept the ticket stand for anyone loitering in the shadows, "night before last somebody discovered the lion's cage unlatched."

"A lion?" Amy Jo's eyes widened.

Becky's jaw dropped open. "Unlatched?"

25

"Mr. Barney was hopping mad about it, too," he continued. "But the night that it happened the lion trainer swears it was locked when he checked it. Lucky for us the lion didn't push against the door and get out. He was sound asleep when the trainer made his midnight check. It's making everybody edgy, though, I can tell you that."

"Hm," said Amy Jo, looking slyly at her friend. "I told you something was going on here."

Becky shrugged her shoulders as she explained to Ernie. "She loves to pretend she's Sherlock Holmes."

"Well," said Ernie, looking at them doubtfully, "I'd be careful . . . you two girls might be biting off more than you can chew."

Amy Jo straightened her shoulders. "Don't worry," she said confidently. "We'll have a look around and let you know what we find out."

Ernie blinked his eyes a few times and scratched behind his ear as he stared at Amy Jo.

Becky drew in her breath slowly as the girls turned to leave. "See you tomorrow, Ernie," she said.

Oreo and Ginger bobbed their heads up and down as Becky and Amy Jo reached the paddock. The ponies walked to the fence and stretched their necks over the gate to take a piece of candy from the girls' outstretched hands.

"The candy makes their breath smell like peppermint," Becky smiled as she unwrapped another piece for her pony.

Amy Jo stroked Ginger's face absentmindedly. "What do you think of the story Ernie gave us about Andy?"

"What do you mean?" asked Becky with a knowing sigh.

Amy Jo frowned in concentration.  "We didn't actually see a clown around the Ferris wheel. We only have Ernie's word that there actually *was* a clown."

Becky shook her head. "You're imagination's working overtime."

"You don't know that," said Amy Jo defensively. "Anyway, somebody doesn't want us around the circus, that's for sure."

"Why are you so suspicious?" asked Becky, as she slipped into the saddle. "What happened might have been an accident."

Amy Jo gave Becky a wilting look as she turned in her saddle. "That'll be the first place we look," she said as she nodded at the trailer where the woman had stood in the window. "Let's get here a little earlier tomorrow and have a look around, maybe find out who she is."

CHAPTER 4

Her Name's Zelda

Mr. Ferrell glanced up as the girls stepped through the door the following afternoon. He stifled a yawn as they walked towards his desk.

Poor man is probably working too hard and not getting enough sleep, thought Becky.

Wonder what he's been up to that he's staying out so late, thought Amy Jo.

Becky handed the assistant an envelope. "It's Mr. Barney's share of the money from the pony rides last night," she said.

"Okay, I'll see that he gets it," said Mr. Ferrell as he slipped the envelope into a side drawer. He gave them a brief nod, reached for his pen, and bent over his work.

Amy Jo gave a sidelong glance to Becky and cleared her throat. "Sure is a nice riding ring you have over there."

"Thanks," said Mr. Ferrell, without looking up.

"Not many trailers over there either," Amy Jo continued.

"No," he responded.

"Just one, actually," she commented, tapping the tips of her fingers together. "Thought you said it was empty."

When Mr. Ferrell didn't answer, she pressed on. "Wonder who lives there?"

Mr. Ferrell looked up. "Why do you want to know?"

"Well, uh," said Amy Jo, caught off guard, but only for a second, "we'll be neighbors, sort of, and it wouldn't be neighborly not to know who our neighbors are."

"I see," said Mr. Ferrell as he went back to his work. "Her name's Zelda."

Amy Jo raised her eyebrows and widened her eyes as she looked at Becky and mouthed the word "Zelda." "Okay, thanks," she stammered slightly. "We'll be seeing you."

"Right," he answered as they closed the screen door on their way out.

"I can't *believe* how you worm answers out of people," said Becky, as they made their way back to the ponies. "I mean I'm such a chicken. I'd have just melted and slithered out of there when he asked me why I wanted to know."

"I was like that when I first got into the detective business, too, but now I just nose my way in and ask what I want to know," replied Amy Jo.

Ginger and Oreo shook their heads as the girls reached the place where they were tied. Today, the mares had only waited a short time, not much chance to nibble on grass.

The girls gathered the reins in their hands and started walking towards the riding ring. Amy Jo gave out a short laugh. "Zelda?! Can you believe we're working right nextdoor to Zelda?" Her eyes lit up mischievously. "I wonder what she was doing last night that she didn't want us to see."

"Why do you always think people are trying to hide something?" asked Becky. "She was probably just changing her clothes or something. It's still early. Let's stop and get some ice cream."

Amy Jo perked up. "All right," she said, momentarily forgetting their case.

Amy Jo's face dropped a bit when she spied Paige behind the counter. "Probably making money hand over fist," she muttered to Becky.

"Lighten up, Amy Jo," said Becky. "She's our friend. Anyway, we have jobs, too, now."

"Okay, okay," replied Amy Jo, feeling only the tiniest bit embarrassed.

"May I help you?" said Paige in that slightly superior voice that one who has a job reserves for someone who doesn't.

Not one to be outdone, Amy Jo replied equally haughtily. "Well, we don't have much time because we have to be at work in a few minutes."

Becky ignored both of them. "Fudge ripple, please," she said. Oreo nudged Becky's arm. "Oh, and strawberry for Oreo."

Paige stared at both girls. "How did you get a job so fast?" she asked. "Yesterday morning you hadn't even started looking."

Amy Jo puffed out her chest, but only slightly. "We're giving pony rides over at the riding ring," she said, pointing in the direction of the big top. "Must have given a hundred rides last night, wouldn't you

31

say, Beck?" continued Amy Jo, stretching the numbers just a bit.

Becky ignored the drift of the conversation. "One fudge ripple and one strawberry, please," she repeated.

"A hundred rides?!" Paige was impressed.

Amy Jo puffed out her chest just a little bit more. "Well, we were pretty tired, but what's total exhaustion when you have a job you just love. That's what I always say."

Becky looked at both of them. "Do you two mind if I get some ice cream?" she asked.

Both girls turned to her and with a flutter Paige picked up her ice cream dipper. "Oh, sure, Becky," she said flipping up the lid on the freezer. "What'll it be?"

For the third time Becky repeated her order. "One fudge ripple and one strawberry," she demanded. She'd already said "please" twice and that was enough. Then, turning to Amy Jo, she asked, "What are you going to get?"

"Ah, hm," said Amy Jo as she studied the menu. "All the words are written with a backwards slant. I wonder who wrote this?"

"I did," responded Paige as she handed Becky two cones. "Hank gave me a list of the flavors he was bringing out here and I wrote it out on that board."

Becky held out the strawberry ice cream for Oreo to nibble while she licked her fudge ripple cone. "By the way, where is Hank?"

"He had to go back to the store and get some more ice cream," Paige explained. "I'm in charge while he's gone," she explained proudly.

"Hm," said Amy Jo again as she
traced the letters on the menu. "Why do
you slant the letters backward?"

"I'm left handed," Paige explained, leaning on the
counter. "My teacher is trying to fix it, but I don't really care. I
got better things to do than worry about my handwriting."

"I see," said Amy Jo, logging that information
away for future reference. "Well, let me think now," she
continued, finally ready to order. "I'll take chocolate chip
cookie dough for me and vanilla for Ginger," she added,
looking at Ginger.

"Oh," said Paige, taken aback. "That's the flavor
Hank went back to get. We don't have chocolate chip
cookie dough right now."

"No chocolate chip cookie dough?" asked Amy
Jo in dismay. "Oh, well, just give me two vanillas."

"That'll be four dollars," said Paige as she deposited two cones into Amy Jo's outstretched hands. "That
cup right beside the napkins is for tips."

"Tips, huh," said Amy Jo as she firmly deposited
her change into her pocket.

Becky looked pointedly at Amy Jo, then placed a
quarter in the cup and smiled at Paige. "You did a very
good job," she began. "Thank you very much. We'll be
back tomorrow."

Amy Jo licked her ice cream for a moment then
reached in her pocket. "Yeah, you did a nice job," she
added ruefully as she tossed a dime in the cup.

The girls gave their ponies the last crumbs of the
cones then led them towards the riding ring. Every few
steps Ginger nudged Amy Jo in the back. Where's my
ice cream? she seemed to say.

33

Not to be outdone, Oreo snorted her disappointment. Both ponies really started to balk as the riding ring came into view.

"Hi-ho, hi-ho, it's off to work we go," recited Amy Jo, feeling in league with the ponies.

"A few minutes ago you were bragging about having a job," teased Becky.

"Yeah, well," Amy Jo began as she eyed the line up of kids waiting to take a pony ride. "Let's just get to it."

*   *   *   *

The last rays of the sun peeked over the horizon as the girls closed the gate to the paddock after pony rides were over for the evening.

"You know," Amy Jo began, her body sagging against the gate then sliding to the ground, "I sort of liked that old paper route. I don't know why I ever let you talk me out of asking for another route after Andy and Jenny came back. Maybe if we were real nice to the circulation manager, he'd give us another route."

"You've sure got a short memory," said Becky, shaking her head. "You hated getting up at five-thirty in the morning as much as I did," she continued as she plopped down beside her friend.

"Remember Mrs. Martin?" Amy Jo continued. "She used to put chocolate chip cookies on the front porch for us."

Becky folded her arms. "I remember one morning it was so dark you didn't see them and stepped right in the middle of the plate. I was hungry that morning, too!"

"Easy for you to laugh," Amy Jo  scoffed. "You weren't the one who had to clean off the plate so Mrs. Martin would think we ate her cookies. I had to hop off the porch so my chocolaty shoe wouldn't make tracks on the step and give us away!"

Becky tried to speak but fell to the side laughing.

Amy Jo shook her head, her eyes crinkling at the corners. As she looked beyond the paddock, a frown crept in around the edges. "Beck," she said in a low voice, "look who just stepped out of Zelda's trailer."

Becky turned her head and followed Amy Jo's gaze. "It's a clown."

Amy Jo studied the retreating figure. "We saw Zelda leave for the big top while we were giving pony rides," she said. "She wouldn't have time to change into a clown suit and then change back in time for the knife-throwing act, would she?"

Becky frowned for a few seconds. "Maybe somebody sneaked into her trailer. I wonder if it's the same clown that Ernie was talking about last night."

"I was thinking the same thing." Amy Jo took Becky's arm and led her around the corner of the paddock. "Come on, let's tail whomever it is and see what's going on."

"Well," Becky swallowed hard, "let's not get too close; we don't want to give ourselves away."

"No sweat," said Amy Jo as they reached the first tent. "The suspect doesn't stand a chance when I'm around."

CHAPTER 5

The Lighter Fluid Can

"We lost him," said Becky, a hint of relief in her voice.

"We didn't lose him." Amy Jo was defensive. "We just don't know where he is, that's all."

Becky rolled her eyes and turned to go back to the paddock.

"Hey!" Amy Jo stopped her. "Do you smell that?"

Becky sniffed the air. "It smells like lighter fluid," she said softly. "Where's it coming from?"

Amy Jo lifted her head in the air, sniffing in all directions. "I don't know. Let's work our way towards the center and see if we can find out."

"Okay," said Becky, feeling as though they were in over their heads already. "I hope this doesn't take long."

As the girls stepped over wires and cables, the scent of lighter fluid grew stronger. The sound of someone rushing over gravel brought them to a halt. They edged up to the next tent and peered around the corner. The door to a small, white trailer had been propped open. A clown held a metal container and stood over a stack of costumes piled on the gravel.

When Amy Jo leaned forward to get a better look, the clown stiffened and turned slightly, as though suddenly aware of being watched. The girls shot back, dropped to the ground, and frantically wiggled under the bottom of the tent.

The gloved hands tossed the lighter fluid can aside. Footsteps circled the tent twice, then they returned to the stack of costumes.

The girls slowly heaved a sigh of relief. There was only blackness inside the tent. Even after their eyes had adjusted to the darkness, they could see nothing. It was hot and close without the flap open. Beads of sweat trickled down their backs, yet their mouths were dry.

Amy Jo got on her hands and knees and began to crawl. "Come on," she whispered over her shoulder. "Grab hold of my pant leg and we'll move to the front. Maybe we can lift the bottom of the tent enough to see what's going on."

Becky's voice creaked at first. "Okay," she finally uttered. "I'll try."

"Grab hold!" whispered Amy Jo again.

"I *am* holding," Becky insisted.

"I don't know what you're holding, but it's not my pant leg." Amy Jo groped around until she found Becky's hand. "Oh, yuck," she said as her hand touched something cold and slimy.

"Oh, no," Becky whined softly. "It's disgusting and I can't even wash it off."

"Well, don't think about what it might be," Amy Jo said, wiping her hand on the bottom of the tent. "Just hold on and let's go."

They inched forward, then they slowly lifted the bottom of the tent and peered under the flap.

A match had been struck. The small flame flickered in the evening breeze and the clown's right hand came up to shield it.

The hand slowly lowered the match to the pile of costumes then dropped it the last few inches. The costumes immediately burst into flames. The smell of lighter fluid was stronger now. The growing wind quickly took the odor to the far end of the circus.

The clown slowly stood up. There was something about the face. It wasn't right. The mouth should have been turned up in a smile, but it was slanted down. And two huge painted teardrops had been formed just under each eye. Those eyes continued to stare unblinkingly into the flames as if in a trance. The clown's entire body shivered as if awakening from a deep sleep into a place that was very cold. After one last look around, the clown picked up the metal can and melted into the darkness.

"Come on!" said Amy Jo, as she forced her way through the bottom of the tent. "He's getting away!"

"Wait for me!" answered Becky, struggling to free herself from the bottom of the tent.

This way! Amy Jo's wild motions seem to say.

Becky tripped over a tent peg hidden in the shadows and flipped over on her side. "O-oh," she moaned.

Amy Jo raced back, grabbed her under the arm, and jerked her to her feet. "Not so loud," she hissed as she dragged her friend along at full speed. "You'll give us away."

Becky gulped down untimely tears and hobbled along. "Injured in the line of duty," she mumbled to herself. "As if anybody cares."

They came to a small clearing. Nothing.

Amy Jo whirled around and stamped her foot. "This is not going to happen twice in one evening," she said quietly but with determination. "You go that way and I'll go this way and we'll meet on the other side of that trailer," she finished, then circled to the right while Becky stumbled somewhat shakily to the left.

They met in the middle of a long trailer and stood still while Amy Jo plotted their next move. Becky opened her mouth to call it quits. But before she got the first word out, they heard the sound of someone rushing past on the opposite side of them.

"Let's go!" Amy Jo whispered as she turned on her heel and began to sprint.

They spotted the clown running under a security light as they rounded the next corner. The girls kept up the chase, but in a crouched-down position.

Suddenly, the clown stopped. Amy Jo slid behind the cover of a tent and Becky slid right after her.

Amy Jo muffled a cry of pain and grabbed her leg. "I wish you wouldn't slam right into me," she whispered.

"Sorry," Becky mumbled an apology. "Being your sidekick can be dangerous," she continued softly. "People get hurt and it's usually not the suspect either."

Amy Jo opened her mouth to reply when she heard the sound of metal landing on a pile of cans. The noise echoed around the tents and trailers.

"Sounds like the lighter fluid can got thrown on top of something," Amy Jo whispered, scooting closer to the corner.

They heard retreating footsteps and jumped up. "Quick, he's getting away!" Amy Jo said, limping the first few steps.

"Why do you keep saying 'he'?  What makes you think it's a man?" Becky called, forgetting to lower her voice.

Amy Jo suddenly felt overwhelmingly weary. "I don't know really," she answered, deciding to give up the chase. "I guess I'm still thinking of him as 'Andy the clown.' We might as well forget it. He's too far away anyway. Let's look for that can."

"Must have tossed it into this dumpster," said Becky as she eyed the huge, green, metal container.

"Wish I could be sure it's in there," Amy Jo muttered, looking around for a way to step onto something and take a look over the edge.

"Why don't I kneel down and you can step onto my shoulders?" Becky suggested.

"Okay," said Amy Jo as she put a foot on Becky's shoulder.

"Careful!" shouted Becky. "You're stepping on my hair!"

Amy Jo lifted her foot. "Well, move your hair out of the way." She repositioned one foot on Becky's shoulder, then she carefully placed the second foot on the other shoulder. For a second she felt balanced, but her knees began to wobble, her arms flailed like propellers, and she fell backwards squarely on her behind.

"This isn't going to work," said Becky, massaging her shoulders.

"I know," said Amy Jo, rubbing the back of her jeans. "Okay, why don't you get on your hands and knees and I'll try standing on your back."

Becky took a deep breath and let it out cautiously. "All right, just don't step on my fingers."

"Don't worry," Amy Jo held up her right hand the way she'd seen witnesses do on TV when they swear to tell the truth in court. "I will not step on your fingers."

Placing her hands on the dumpster for balance, Amy Jo gently stepped on Becky's back and peered over the edge. "The light's a little dim, but it looks like the same can," she said, then stepped down.

"Did you get a good look at it before it was thrown in there?"

"Good enough to be sure that's the one," Amy Jo answered.

Becky stood up and brushed the dirt off her knees. "Okay, we'd better head back now."

Suddenly, the cry of neighing horses and the sound of pounding hooves filled the air.

"The gate!" Amy Jo's eyes were on Becky. "We latched it. I'm sure of it."

"Oreo and Ginger!" Becky cried as they broke into a run.

CHAPTER 6

Breaking and Entering

Six white horses galloped towards the girls as they entered the clearing. Amy Jo grabbed Becky's arm and shoved her back as the horses stampeded past, their manes and tails flying in the air.

Oreo and Ginger were well behind the pack, but "herd instinct" had lured them to race after the horses. The girls stepped in front of their ponies, arms out from their sides.

"Whoa, girl," Amy Jo called, ready to jump to the side if Ginger decided not to stop.

"Easy, Oreo," Becky said soothingly, reaching into her pocket for candy.

Sweat glistened on the backs and sides of the mares. The whites of their eyes could be seen in the dim light. For a moment, it looked as though they were going to continue to follow the pack. But at the last second, the mares broke into a trot and began to circle the girls.

"Whoa, girl," Amy Jo called again. "Slow down, now."

Becky turned in a circle as her pony continued to trot around her. "Here, girl, come on, now," Becky cooed, stretching her hand out so that Oreo could see the candy.

The ponies trotted in a circle several more times before shifting to a walk.

The girls removed their belts and trailed after them. The ponies finally came to a halt when they smelled the candy.

"Easy, girl," said Becky, as she edged her way toward Oreo, who was snorting and pawing the ground.

"Come on, Ginger," Amy Jo said softly. The pony tossed her head and looked longingly after the running horses. "Just a few more steps, girl, and everything will be all right."

The ponies reached out towards the candy and nibbled it off the girls' hands.

"Starburst mints taste pretty good, don't they, Ginger!" said Amy Jo sighing with relief.

They fed the mares candy with one hand and slipped the belt around their necks with the other hand. A makeshift lead rope was created by looping one end of the belt through the buckle.

The mares balked at being led back to the paddock but yielded after another piece of candy was offered.

The girls placed the halters and lead ropes on their ponies and tied them to the paddock fence. The girths had just been attached to the right side of the saddles when a man walked towards them, leading one of the white horses.

The girls had never seen him before. From the look on his face they weren't too crazy about meeting him now either.

"Do you girls know anything about the horses getting out?" he demanded.

Becky shook her head. "No, I don't know anything about it."

"How about you?" He nodded at Amy Jo.

"I didn't see anything either," she said, stealing a quick look at Becky. "Do you think somebody left the

46

gates unlatched by accident?" she asked bravely.

"Not a chance," he answered firmly. "I was here about ten minutes ago and they were latched then. Which means," he continued, "that someone unlatched them on purpose." He leaned forward and looked sternly at the girls. "Know anything about that?"

"Not a thing," Amy Jo assured him.

"All I know is that they were latched when we left," Becky added convincingly.

"Anyway," Amy Jo continued, "we'd never do anything like that."

"I didn't think so," he said, still looking at them. "At least, I hope not. All right, girls," he added, after closing the gate. "I've got to help round up the rest of the horses."

Amy Jo grew quiet as she threw the reins over Ginger's head. "Whoever let the horses out knew that everyone would be busy with the fire."

"So you think that the fire was just a distraction so they could turn the horses loose?"

"I don't know," Amy Jo answered. "Maybe it's a plot to create as much trouble as possible."

"Why would anybody want to set a fire and then let the horses out?" Becky asked.

"For that matter, why would anybody unlatch the lion's cage?" Amy Jo answered her with another question.

They finished tacking up the ponies in silence. By now the ponies were calm and stood still. Ginger, who usually turned her head as though she would nip, stood still while her girth was being tightened. The girls mounted the mares and turned their heads towards home.

After pressing Ginger into a trot, Amy Jo said, "Tomorrow, let's find out whose costumes got burned."

"What about the clown?" Becky asked as she caught up with her friend.

"Yeah, I've been thinking about the clown," said Amy Jo, eyeing Zelda's trailer with suspicion as they rode past it. "It seems like that trailer might be a good place to start. I've been wondering what's going on inside there," she murmured half to herself.

"You wouldn't . . .?" Becky's eyes widened. "I mean, you wouldn't . . . snoop?"

"I wouldn't call it snooping, exactly. More like . . ." Amy Jo struggled for just the right word. "More like watching out for your neighbors," she finished, pleased that she'd found just the right phrase.

"Watching out for your neighbors?" Becky repeated in disbelief.

Amy Jo shifted in her saddle. "Suppose I saw some stranger in a disguise coming out of your house when you weren't there. I mean, dressed like a clown for instance," she began slowly. "Now, what kind of neighbor would I be if I didn't look into it, huh? I mean they might walk out with something that's really important, like a . . . a diamond watch or something."

"We don't have any diamond watches at our house." Becky pulled back slightly on her reins, slowing Oreo down to a walk

"Walk, Ginger." Amy Jo squeezed her legs for support and sat deeper into her saddle. "Well, what if you *did* have a diamond watch and this guy was trying to steal it? I'd need to check it out, right? So, I figure I ought to do that for Zelda, too. I mean people are sneaking in and out

48

of her trailer. Wouldn't be neighborly not to  look into it for her." Smugness had seeped into her voice. Goodwill and best intentions were written all over her face. "In fact, it would be my good deed for the day."

Becky heaved a great sigh. It was useless to try to talk her friend out of this. The issue now was . . . damage control. "Okay, so when are you going to *sneak* into her trailer?"

Amy Jo gave her friend a piercing look for her choice of words. "After dark tomorrow night," she said, deciding not to argue about it. "No sense having the glare and heat of the sun on our heads. Besides," she thought out loud, "don't want a lot of nosy parkers thinking we're breaking and entering. After we turn the ponies loose in the paddock, we'll walk over to Zelda's trailer."

Becky covered her face and muttered, "Third day on the job and we're breaking and entering."

"On the other hand," Amy Jo continued thoughtfully, totally ignoring Becky's misgivings, "maybe we'd better keep the ponies saddled nearby, in case Zelda comes back and doesn't realize we're trying to help her out. Folks can be a little funny like that sometimes."

Becky closed her eyes and shivered at the thought of Zelda catching them rummaging through her trailer. "Can't we just forget about this and go home after the pony rides are done?" she pleaded.

Amy Jo shook her head. "Look, Beck, I'll be in and out of there in a flash. You hold the ponies and be the lookout and I'll go in and sn . . ., I mean investigate. Then we'll go home."

Becky slumped in her saddle. "Okay, I'll hold the ponies, you go as fast as you can, and then we'll leave."

CHAPTER 7

Click, Thump

As they drew the ponies near Zelda's trailer the following evening, Amy Jo looked over her shoulder then eyed Becky closely. "Okay, you keep watch while I look around inside," she said, handing her friend the end of Ginger's reins.

Becky stood quaking next to the trailer as both mares sniffed her pockets. "So, what are you going to look for?" asked Becky as Oreo nibbled at her jeans.

Amy Jo thought, but only for a second. "I don't exactly know yet," she answered, reaching for the door.

"What if somebody's in there?"

"Oh!" Amy Jo began stroking Ginger's muzzle, worried that her pony might neigh when she left her to go into the trailer. "I'll knock and see if anybody answers."

"What are you going to say if somebody comes to the door?" asked Becky, twisting away to keep Oreo from tearing a hole in her pocket. Her mother had warned that the next time the mare tore a hole in her pocket, Becky could repair it herself.

"If somebody opens the door, I'll think of something." Amy Jo rapped several times and waited.

"This is just great!" muttered Becky, looking anxiously in every direction.

"Don't worry," Amy Jo assured her friend after thirty seconds. "Nobody's in there, so I'm going in."

"What if somebody comes while you're inside?" asked Becky, desperate to go home and put an end to this madness.

"What if, what if, what if," Amy Jo answered. "Knock twice and stall them."

"How am I going to do that holding both of these ponies?" asked Becky, but Amy Jo had already slipped inside. "Oh, I'll tie them around the corner and come back," she muttered to herself.

Bright lights surrounded a large mirror with pots and tubes of make-up spilling over the table in front of it. Long, sequined dresses with low necks and rounded backs hung on hooks. High heeled shoes had been tossed in a corner on the floor.

What am I looking for, Amy Jo thought as her eyes wandered around the trailer. She walked over to the costumes and pushed them aside. Her hands probed behind them, hoping to find a mysterious, hidden door. Everything seemed pretty solid. Frowning, she arranged everything as it was before, then she turned away and headed for the pile of shoes in the corner.

Maybe there's a secret compartment hidden in the heel or something. Amy Jo bent down and began twisting and pressing on the shoes. *Nothing here either,* she sighed. Shrugging her shoulders she stood up.

She studied the dressing table. There were two long pieces of cloth tacked around the edge of it with a slit in the front forming a skirt. *Hm,* she thought, as she moved towards it.

Suddenly, Amy Jo heard a gruff, raspy voice from outside. "What are you doing hanging around this trailer?!"

"Well," she heard Becky reply. "Well, I was just, I mean, uh . . ."

"Get lost, kid," he said, then opened the trailer door.

From under the table, Amy Jo stilled the ends of the skirt with shaking hands just before the visitor turned around from shutting the door. Her pulse beat against the hollow of her throat, while beads of sweat trickled down her face. As the man walked past the slit in the skirt, Amy Jo's eyes widened and she covered her mouth to keep from making any sound. It was the blue-and-red-striped clown costume from last night!

The clown immediately changed clothes and threw his costume into a large bag. His shoes came off next and they were tossed in the same bag as the costume. Amy Jo's breathing stopped as he headed over to the dressing table.

He sat down and slipped his feet into another pair of shoes. Then he turned around and shoved his legs under the table. Amy Jo quietly drew her legs closer to her body and leaned nearer the wall. She heard him open a jar, grab tissues, and mutter under his breath, "Nosy brat. Wonder where the other one is."

As the clown leaned forward to check his face in the mirror, he shifted his feet, almost brushing Amy Jo's shoe. Then he dabbed on more cream and removed the last trace of make-up with another tissue. He turned around in the chair and stood up. "Okay, I'm out of here," he said, grabbing the bag with his clown costume.

Amy Jo looked down at the back of his shoes. One of them had a metal cleat on the heel; the cleat on the other heel was missing.

Click, thump, click, thump his shoes echoed on the linoleum as he walked to the door. Amy Jo leaned towards the slit then pulled back. *He might turn around at the last minute.*

*   *   *   *

"Some lookout you are!" said Amy Jo, stepping out of the trailer a few minutes later.

"I'm telling you, he just appeared out of nowhere," Becky's voice was an octave higher than usual. "I didn't see him coming and all of a sudden he was right in front of me."

Amy Jo sensed that her friend was at the edge and ready to spill over. "Don't worry; it's okay," she answered, placing her hand gently on her friend's arm. "Did you get a look at him when he left?"

Becky took a deep breath. "I was around the corner with Oreo and Ginger and didn't see him leave," she answered, gaining control.

"All right, well, let's get the ponies and ride out of here before he comes back again," said Amy Jo, leading the way.

Becky looked over at Amy Jo. "Did you find anything?"

"No, but he said something kind of strange."

"What?"

"He said, 'Wonder where the other one is,'" Amy Jo repeated from memory.

Becky frowned. "What did he  mean by that?"

"He must have recognized you and knew that the two of us are always together," Amy Jo began patiently. "So he wondered where I was and why I wasn't with you."

"That's sort of scary," said Becky slowly.

"I know," Amy Jo agreed nervously. "This is a pretty big place, but he's seen us, which means it's probably someone we've already met."

The ponies neighed and shook their heads as they saw the girls approaching. Their eyes seemed to ask, Is this all we get after a hard night's work?

Becky looked sympathetically at her pony. "Poor Oreo, you want to go home, too, don't you?"

Amy Jo slipped her hand in her pocket and as soon as Ginger heard the crinkling of paper, she began to nod her head and edge nearer. "Here you go, Ginger," she said, holding out her hand. "I'm sorry we made you wait so long. We'll take you home and give you some nice hay and feed."

"We have to tell Mr. Barney about this," said Becky, turning her pony around. "Maybe we should ride into the village tomorrow morning and talk to Officer Higgins."

Amy Jo's eyes had lost their sparkle. "We haven't found out very much, so there's not much to tell Officer Higgins. He'll just tell us to stay out of it. That's what he always says," Amy Jo continued bitterly.

Becky's face lit up for the first time that night. "That's not a bad idea," she said. "Maybe we should!"

Amy Jo looked at her partner with a mixture of pity and disgust. "Let's just start with Mr. Barney for now," she said. "We'll come here early tomorrow and stop in the office." They rode in silence for a few moments. "There's something we haven't thought of," she continued quietly.

"What's that?" asked Becky wearily.

Amy Jo turned to her friend as they past the last security light. "What if Mr. Barney's in on this?"

Becky let that piece of information sink in then asked. "Why would he be in on it?"

Amy Jo shook her head. "I don't know," she admitted. "Maybe there's insurance money or maybe he has a grudge against somebody. Who knows? But it would be real easy for him to be anywhere on the circus grounds without raising suspicion."

Becky looked really confused now. "Well, what should we do then?"

Amy Jo rode on in silence for a time. "We'll just have to take our chances and tell him what we've found," she finally decided. "We gotta remember two things."

"What's that?"

"We don't know anybody here and we don't trust anybody either."

CHAPTER 8

One Knife Is Missing

Mr. Ferrell was busy scribbling something on a piece of paper when the girls walked through the door the following morning.

"Is Mr. Barney in?" Amy Jo asked as they reached his desk.

Mr. Ferrell looked up. "Yes, but he's on the telephone now," he answered, checking the light on his telephone that indicated that his boss was still on the line. "Can I help you?"

"Not really," Becky answered. "Here's his share of the money from last night."

"Okay," he said, putting it into the same drawer as yesterday. "I'll give it to him."

"Uh," Amy Jo said, sneaking a look at Becky. "Know anything about the fire?"

Mr. Ferrell glanced up and studied both of them. "No, nothing. Why do you want to know?" he asked slowly.

"Oh, well, just thought I'd ask," said Amy Jo.

Mr. Ferrell continued to stare at them.

The girls began to step backwards towards the door.

"Well, guess we'll be moving along," said Amy Jo as they reached the screen door.

The girls watched as the early morning circus came alive. Coffee was being served at a nearby stand and Ernie sat alone at a table sipping from a cup.

Amy Jo nodded in his direction. "Let's see what we can find out," she said, stepping away from the manager's trailer.

The girls bought a cup of hot chocolate at the stand and wandered slowly over to where Ernie sat.

"Too bad about the fire last night," said Amy Jo as they sat down opposite him.

Ernie seemed a bit startled and looked quickly around to see if anyone was watching. He cleared his throat. "Yep," he answered, but he squirmed a bit as if he weren't too happy to see them.

Amy Jo took a breath and started again. "Any idea whose costumes they were?"

Ernie took another sip of his coffee. "Zorbon's stuff is what I hear," he offered reluctantly.

"Oh!" Becky's eyes widened. "You mean that knife thrower?"

"Yeah," Ernie responded. He studied the girls for a moment then continued. "That happened pretty late, didn't get in the papers yet either," he said frowning. "How'd you girls hear about it?"

"Oh! Well, uh," Amy Jo stuttered. "We just happened to be hanging around last night, that's all."

"Hm," Ernie said. He eyed them suspiciously over the rim of his coffee cup. "I gotta leave. Have to see Mr. Barney now."

The girls watched Ernie walk quickly towards the manager's trailer then got up and headed back to where the ponies were tied.

"I suppose he thinks we had something to do with it," worried Becky as they mounted their ponies and guided them past the Ferris wheel. It would be a long time before they'd ever set foot on that ride again.

"Works both ways," commented Amy Jo.

"Do you think he might have done it?" asked Becky.

"I don't think we should rule out anyone for now," answered Amy Jo.

Becky leaned forward and gave Oreo a pat on the neck. "May as well go home and do our morning chores," she decided.

"Yeah," Amy Jo agreed as they trotted towards Main Street and Bedford. "Haven't mucked out the stalls or cleaned the water buckets yet. And Ginger's water bucket gets so disgusting it has to be cleaned out everyday. Every morning it looks like that green stuff at the edge of the pond behind your house."

As they turned left onto Park Avenue, Amy Jo pinched her lips together. "That's a little strange, don't you think?"

Becky shook her head and sighed. "Now what?"

"Well," said Amy Jo, ignoring her friend's comment, "don't you think it's strange that *Ernie* knows whose costumes got burned, but Mr. Barney's assistant doesn't have a clue?"

"That is pretty odd." Becky thought a second. "I wonder if Ernie *did* have something to do with it after all?"

Amy Jo nodded her head. "I wonder where he was last night?" she questioned. "And we still only have his word that the clown stopped the Ferris wheel and not him."

"Maybe he's the clown," Becky said in a rare moment of insight.

Amy Jo looked quickly at her friend. "Not bad," she commented, nodding her head in approval. "Not bad at all."

They rode along in silence for a few more moments. As they reached Quarry Road, Amy Jo turned to her friend. "I don't know if we'll find out anything, but let's go to the big top tonight and check out Zorbon."

"All right. It'll be a nice change from breaking and entering," Becky returned sarcastically.

*   *   *   *

The big top rocked with excitement as Becky and Amy Jo paid for their tickets and walked inside. The audience was packed and there was standing room only.

"Let's try to get as close to the front as we can," Amy Jo yelled in Becky's ear. "I want to see how he throws his knife . . . especially when he puts that blindfold on."

Becky grabbed hold of Amy Jo's shirt as they weaved their way through the crowd. Disgruntled remarks followed them, but finally there was no one between them and the ring. "Look over there," she shouted, pointing her finger. "They're coming out."

Amy Jo nodded her head as her eyes followed the pair's ascent to the platform. A table was positioned on the left side. At the other end stood a round, wooden wheel which stood about six feet tall. It had two  straps at the top for Zelda's arms and two straps at the bottom for her legs.

The audience applauded and whistled as Zorbon the Great and Zelda took their first bow. Zorbon's teeth seemed huge and white against his dark skin. His powerful arms were hidden under his white shirt. Dangling from his neck was a silver chain with a miniature knife which swung with each step he took.

Zelda turned her head and looked directly into Amy Jo's eyes. She wore a shimmering emerald dress. A perfect match to the cool, green eyes that stared at the young detective.

Amy Jo felt a chill creep through her body even after Zelda's gaze moved past her. She glanced at Becky, but Zorbon was absorbing all of her friend's attention.

A hush fell over the audience as Zorbon escorted his assistant to the wheel, then walked to the table where a dozen gleaming knives were lined up waiting. He passed his hands over the table, touching several before finally selecting one. Snatching up a piece of paper in his left hand, he raised both arms, and turned to the crowd. He placed the knife at the top of the paper. In seconds, the paper was slit into small pieces. The crowd went wild. A pleased, haughty smile that he saved for the audience flashed onto Zorbon's face, then he turned back to the table.

"Here it comes," said Becky, steeling herself.

"Yeah, here it comes," echoed Amy Jo, her eyes glued to the wooden wheel.

Knife in hand, Zorbon studied the wheel, taking aim. He drew his arm back, lunged forward, and released.

The knife sliced through the air, missing his assistant's left hand by inches. People in the audience dragged their eyes away from Zelda and watched Zorbon study the remaining eleven knives on the table.

The girls exchanged glances. They didn't know if their nerves could hold out for the next eleven throws.

Zorbon selected another knife, pulled his arm slowly back, and lunged again. This time the knife landed just beside her knee. Zorbon walked over to his assistant and fastened clips around her body, securing her to the wheel. Then, he reached to the side and turned on a switch. The wheel slowly began to turn. Every time the wheel made a complete revolution there was a clicking sound which let Zorbon know where the wheel was in its cycle.

Amy Jo's eyes widened as she leaned forward. Her head nodded to the rhythm of the clicking sound.

This time Zorbon grabbed the first three knives in line. He took quick aim and fired one after the other at the rotating wheel. Each one landed closer to her body than the one before.

At last, he turned to the audience and with a flourish, drew out a large, black handkerchief. He covered his eyes with it and tied it behind his head.

The audience fastened their eyes on Zelda and the wheel, half in anticipation, half in horror.

Zorbon groped on the table for a knife, then tilted his head slightly. He drew his arm back slowly, listened for the click, and threw. A sigh rose in the audience as the knife landed safely beside the three-inch heels. Zorbon fumbled for another knife and tilted his head again. His left hand clenched into a fist and relaxed. Perspiration had collected on his forehead and he  reached up to wipe it away.

Amy Jo was puzzled by Zorbon's nervous hesitation. He must have done this a thousand times. Why was he worried now?

Zorbon squared his shoulders, tilted his head, and tuned into the clicking sound of the wheel. He drew back his arm and hurled the knife forward. Zelda screamed. Zorbon tore off his blindfold as the audience rose to its feet.

Zorbon rushed to Zelda's side and flipped off the switch. As soon as he released her from the clasps, she grabbed her shoulder. Blood seeped through her fingers staining her dress. He caught her around the waist as she staggered, then lead her off the platform and out of the tent.

Becky stared, pale-faced, at the retreating figures, then she turned to Amy Jo. "Do you think she's really hurt?"

"I don't know," Amy Jo replied, straining against the rope to watch them leave.

A murmur rose in the audience, children edged closer to their mothers and began to whimper. The jugglers and clowns quickly came into the ring and soon the crowd sat down and began to relax.

Amy Jo stood next to the ring only a few feet from the act. But her forehead creased and her eyes were on the platform that Zorbon and Zelda had just left.

The girls left with the crowd when the show in the big top was over. But as they reached the exit, Amy Jo pulled Becky behind the ticket office and hid until everyone was gone.

"Something's just not right." Amy Jo's eyes looked troubled. "Can you think of anything that seemed kind of strange?"

"Like what?" asked Becky, then shook her head. "I was too upset about her getting hurt to notice anything."

"I can't put my finger on it," Amy Jo called over her shoulder as she headed back inside. "Let's go back in and look around."

"Can't we just go home?" suggested Becky, as she followed Amy Jo into the darkened, empty tent. "What do you want to look for anyway?"

"I don't know, I just want to check stuff out," said Amy Jo looking around.

It seemed strange that only minutes before the tent had been packed. Now, it seemed twice as big, but they were alone. Before, the lights were bright and hot. Now, it was dim and shadowy.

They ducked under the rope separating the audience from the ring and stepped up to the wheel. Amy Jo stretched up on her tiptoes, squinting closely at the spot where Zelda had stood. "No blood where her shoulder would have been," she said. Then she reached over, flipped the switch, and the wheel began to turn.

"Watching this wheel turn is making me dizzy," Becky remarked, turning her back to it.

"Hm, me too," said Amy Jo, then walked over to where Zorbon had stood. She closed her eyes, tilted her head, and listened for the clicks of the turning wheel. "I wonder how he does this?" she puzzled as she opened her eyes and reached towards the knives.

"I hope you're not going to throw them at the

wheel while I'm standing here," Becky
said.

"You won't feel a thing," Amy Jo
teased.

"Very funny," said Becky, making a face.

Amy Jo looked back at the table and studied the
knives. Her fingers reached out and her lips moved si-
lently as she counted them. "Zorbon started out with
twelve knives, right?" asked Amy Jo, looking up.

"Twelve?" Becky thought. "Yeah, twelve."

"Okay, let's figure it out." Amy Jo held up her
hands to tick off the numbers. "He threw the first one
and that landed near her hand." She looked at Becky who
nodded her head. "The second one was near her knee.
Then, he threw three, bang, bang, bang, just like that."

"Right," Becky agreed.

"Okay," Amy Jo continued, having used up five
of her fingers. "Then, he put the blindfold on and threw
one that landed near her shoe and the last one that cut her
shoulder, right?"

"Right."

"And that makes seven, so there should be five
left." Amy Jo raised her eyebrows as she looked at Becky.

Becky looked at Amy Jo's fingers, then she met her
gaze and nodded her head. "Right, there should be five left."

"Well, somebody took one because there are only
four knives here now." Amy Jo beckoned her friend over
to take a look. "One knife is missing."

Becky joined Amy Jo beside the table, her lips
moving as she counted the four remaining knives. She
swallowed as she looked at her friend. "I wonder where
the other knife is?"

"I wonder, too," Amy Jo said, fingering one of the knives.

The sound of the clicking wheel echoed against the canvas walls. The tent vibrated in the wind and the wooden poles supporting it creaked under the strain of holding it up. The cavernous tent felt even more enormous empty than it did filled with people. A few dim security lights created deep shadows in the corners.

Becky looked up at the rows of empty seats. *There are dozens of places where someone could hide*, she thought. "It's creepy in here," she said, clasping her arms around her waist. "Let's turn off the switch and get out of here."

Amy Jo had developed a sudden case of the jitters as well. "Okay," she answered quickly, leading Becky back to the wheel. Just as Amy Jo turned the switch off they heard the echo of footsteps on the wooden floor from somewhere backstage.

Click, thump, click, thump, click, thump.

Amy Jo froze, her eyes wide as she stared at Becky.

Becky grabbed Amy Jo's arms. "Let's get out of here!" she whispered frantically.

Suddenly, a whizzing sound filled the air. Thump! A knife landed between them in the center of the wheel. A note was tied onto its shaft.

Amy Jo let go of Becky's grasping hand long enough to tear the note off. Together, they ran across the ring and ducked under the rope.

CHAPTER 9

The Sign

"We should have tried harder to see Mr. Barney yesterday," said Becky as the two girls walked towards his trailer the following afternoon.

"Well, he was busy and couldn't see us yesterday. Anyway, a lot has happened since then." Amy Jo reached in her pocket for the fourth time to make sure the note was still there. "Now we have something to show him. Whoever wrote it has a lousy backward slant."

"We could have been killed!" Becky insisted.

"Not so loud," Amy Jo cautioned, looking around. "Anyway, he meant to scare us, not kill us."

"How do you know that?" Becky asked.

"Because he knew how to throw a knife. It makes me wonder where Zorbon was when it happened."

As they reached the steps, Zelda stormed out nearly knocking them over. Her eyes looked past them as she swept down the steps.

"Well, don't mind us. We were just standing here," Amy Jo said as the girls turned to watch her walk away.

"Nearly knocked us down, too," said Becky disgustedly.

"She made a pretty quick recovery if you ask me." Amy Jo shrugged her shoulders and continued up the

71

steps. "May we see Mr. Barney?" she asked, as they entered the outer office.

Mr. Ferrell was looking out the window, but turned to the girls as they neared. "I'll check," he said, picking up the telephone and making the request. "Yes, you can go in," he said.

"Thanks," said Becky, then followed Amy Jo towards the manager's office.

Mr. Barney looked up as the girls walked through the door. "You girls bringing in your money from last night?" He smiled, but his eyes looked strained.

"Oh," Becky looked at Amy Jo. "We forgot about that."

"It doesn't matter. Is there something I can do for you then?"

"Uh, well," Amy Jo looked at Becky who was motioning for her to go ahead. "It's like this," she began. "It all started when we got stuck at the top of the Ferris wheel. Not that it was anybody's fault," she added quickly.

"Nobody's fault? I didn't hear anything about this," Mr. Barney said, leaning slightly forward. "Something wrong with the equipment?"

"Not exactly, I mean, that was just the first thing that happened, but we didn't come to talk about that." She looked at Becky who nodded in agreement.

Mr. Barney frowned and pressed his hands together. "I'm a little confused. What exactly is the problem?"

"Well," Amy Jo looked at Becky who urged her on again. "Somebody told us something about a clown the first night, but we didn't know if was true or not. But then we saw him a couple more times, so we're beginning to think that it might be true, but  we're not sure. I mean, we're pretty sure, but not exactly sure."

Mr. Barney stared at Amy Jo for a second, his mouth slightly ajar, then he leaned back in his chair and stared at the ceiling. "Let's see now. There's a situation with the Ferris wheel . . . which you can't talk about. And something about a clown . . . which you're not exactly sure about." He leaned forward placing his arms on the desk. "Just what is it you came to talk about then?"

"This," she said, placing the note on his desk.

Mr. Barney picked up the note and studied it for a few seconds before reading it out loud. "'Quit your pony rides and go home or you'll be sorry.' Where'd you get this?" he asked, looking up at the girls.

"After the show in the big tent last night, we stayed behind to look around," Becky explained.

Mr. Barney pressed his lips together. "Don't you think that was a pretty foolish thing to do? Two young girls all alone in a tent like that?"

"Well, we didn't think there'd be a problem until somebody threw a knife at us!" Amy Jo broke in. "And he threw it like a real pro, too!"

"That's where we got the note," Becky added. "It was tied around the handle of the knife!"

Mr. Barney's eyes narrowed as he looked closely at the girls. "Are you telling me that somebody threw a knife at you with this note tied to it?"

"Yes!" They both said at once.

"You called him a real pro," said Mr. Barney, his voice and face showing the strain of the past week. "Are you accusing Zorbon?"

"We're not sure," Becky answered.

"It's just that whoever threw the knife was really good," Amy Jo suggested.

Becky stretched out her arms. "I mean, we were standing this far apart and he threw it right between us!"

"I see," said Mr. Barney as he began to rub his forehead. "Well, this is very dangerous if what you're saying is true."

Amy Jo leaned her hands on the desk. "It is true. It happened just like we said. And that's not all," she added. "We saw the person who started the fire and where the lighter fluid can got thrown, too."

Mr. Barney jerked his head up and stared at them with bulging eyes. "Who was it?" he asked in a low voice.

Becky shook her head. "We don't know."

"The person was dressed in a clown suit so we couldn't see who it was," Amy Jo explained. "But the lighter fluid can got thrown in that big dumpster."

Mr. Barney sat still for a moment. "I see," he said slowly. "I'll speak to security about this right away." He took out a slip of paper and wrote a few words on it. Swiveling his chair around he looked out the window, and mumbled to himself. "I've checked files and records, hired more security people, and I still can't get to the bottom of this thing." Mr. Barney shook his head and turned his chair back to face the girls again. "Now, I want both of you to stay out of this," he said pointing his finger at them. "Do you hear? You can give your pony rides, but that's all. Okay?" he continued firmly.

"Okay," Becky said meekly.

Amy Jo looked at the floor and sighed, but then nodded her head.

"All right," he said more softly. "Well, I've got to call security so you better run along," Mr. Barney picked up the phone and began to dial. "Oh, thanks for bringing the note to me. And stay out of it," he warned again.

Amy Jo walked out of the trailer into the late afternoon sun her hands stuffed into her pockets. Becky trailed behind her making cooing noises at Oreo only a few yards away, glad to be finally out of the mess.

"You know," said Amy Jo, kicking the pebbles in front of her. "There's something we're missing here. There's something we've seen and I almost think of it, then it goes away."

"Well, don't think of anything now," said Becky as they led their ponies towards the riding ring. "We're off the case, remember? Come on, let's get another ice cream cone. We've got some time before pony rides begin."

"I don't really feel like it, but all right," said Amy Jo, following Becky to the stand.

Paige was busy counting her tips, but looked up when she heard Ginger nicker. "Hi," she said. "More ice cream?"

"Hank running errands again?" asked Becky, looking over the counter.

"Business has been great!" answered Paige. "We ran out of more flavors and he had to run back to town to get them. He was just here a minute ago. He brought double chocolate and peppermint swirl," she continued, as she grabbed a marker and hurried to the sign. "I was suppose to write the new flavors on the sign, but I forgot."

The girls waited patiently as Paige took the lid off the marker and added the two flavors to the board. She slipped behind the counter and picked up the ice cream dipper. "Two cones or four?" she asked, looking at the ponies.

"Fudge ripple for me and strawberry for Oreo," said Becky, laying her money on the counter.

"Did Hank bring chocolate chip cookie dough?" asked Amy Jo. No use asking for what you can't get.

"Sure did," said Paige as she dipped up the first cone.

"Okay, I'll take one of those for me and vanilla for Ginger."

Ginger licked her lips. Oreo stepped forward and sniffed the edge of the counter. Concerned that she'd be edged out, Ginger nudged Oreo out of the way with her head.

"Wait your turn," laughed Becky, pushing both of them gently back.

Amy Jo played with the ends of her reins while she waited for the ice cream cones. Suddenly, she leaned forward and looked at the sign with the flavors written on it. "That's it!" she said, nodding her head. "Yep, that's it, all right."

"What's it?" asked Paige, handing out the last of the ice cream cones.

Becky shook her head. "Don't ask, Paige, 'cause you'll be sorry if she tells you."

"Just look at the sign, Beck!" Amy Jo ignored her partner's comment. "Can't you see? It only makes sense. It couldn't be Zorbon because of the match."

Paige came around from behind the counter and studied the sign. "I don't get it," she said. "What's the matter with the sign?"

"Nothing's the matter with it. In fact, it's a great sign!" exclaimed Amy Jo, giving Paige a brilliant smile. She would have hugged her, but she had no free hands. "Thanks a million, I mean thanks a gazillion! I think you helped us solve the case!" she continued. She turned and led Ginger away, leaving a puzzled Paige to look after them.

"What do you mean it couldn't have been Zorbon because of the match?" asked Becky, trying to lick her ice cream and give Oreo bites of strawberry at the same time.

"He's not left handed," Amy Jo explained as she fed her pony. "Ginger's got ice cream all over her muzzle, what a mess. Anyway, I'm thinking about a couple of things. When I figure them out, we'll go back to Mr. Barney."

CHAPTER 10

The Note

Flashes of lightning pierced the evening sky as the girls made their way to the office after pony rides were over. Thunder rattled from a distance and little swirls of dust eddied around them like a dozen miniature tornadoes.

They stepped up to the screen door and opened it. The inner door had been propped open inside to let in the cooling air.

"May I see Mr. Barney?" asked Amy Jo breathlessly, as they walked up to Mr. Ferrell's desk.

Mr. Ferrell looked at them for a moment before he answered. "Sure, go ahead," he finally said.

Becky watched Amy Jo cross to the manager's office and shut the door behind her. Mr. Ferrell was writing on a tablet of paper . . . no conversation there. Not that Becky wanted to talk to him anyway. She looked around the room, strolled over to the table, and picked up a magazine. It had a picture of circus horses on the front. She glanced at Mr. Ferrell again and decided to sit on the chair behind the door. She snuggled deeply into the cushion and tucked her feet under the chair, making herself as comfy as possible.

Almost immediately the telephone rang and Mr. Ferrell answered it. "Hold on," he said, then he spoke into the intercom. "Mr. Barney, security is calling again."

Seconds later, Mr. Barney came storming out of his office. "I'll have to talk to you later, Amy Jo," he called over his shoulder. "You go on home now. I'll see you tomorrow."

Mr. Barney stopped at his assistant's desk and cleared his throat. "Security found some fingerprints in connection with the fire last night, Karl," he said. "I need you to come along and help me out."

Mr. Ferrell put his pen down and looked up. He crumpled up a piece of paper, tossed it in the direction of the wastebasket, then followed his boss out the door.

After the screen door banged shut, Amy Jo came out of Mr. Barney's office and looked around for Becky. "Where are you?" she finally asked.

"I'm behind the door over here," said Becky, peeking around the edge. "What did Mr. Barney say?"

She shrugged disgustedly. "I didn't get a chance to tell him much. He was on the phone when I walked in. And as soon as he hung up, security called and he left."

"So what do we do now?" Becky asked, settling back in her chair with the magazine again. "Get the ponies and go home?"

"I don't know." Amy Jo began to tap her fingers on top of Mr. Ferrell's desk. The tapping grew slower and slower, then stopped. "Hm," she said. "What's this?"

"What's what?" Becky asked, peeking around the door again.

Amy Jo smoothed out a piece of paper as she walked back into Mr. Barney's office, but returned seconds later holding the note the girls had  brought in earlier that day.

A look of triumphant lit up her face as she strolled towards her partner. "Well, well, what do you know?" she said, as she read the note.

Becky looked up. "What do you mean?"

"Put your magazine down for a minute," Amy Jo directed, as she sat down next to her friend. "Look at the handwriting." She handed her the note from Mr. Barney's office as well as the paper Mr. Ferrell had been writing on when he left.

Becky stared at the note, then at the sheet of paper. "Hm, they're both written with a backward slant. Then she began to read. "Fingerprints found on lighter fluid can. Wait for my phone call at usual time. We'll have to . . ." Becky looked up to meet Amy Jo's gaze.

"Want to know where I got that?" she asked.

Becky gulped. "Where?" she asked, not really wanting to know.

"Behind the wastebasket on the floor beside Mr. Ferrell's desk," answered Amy Jo, triumphantly.

"On the floor?!" Becky was puzzled. "What was it doing there?"

"I don't know. Maybe he was aiming for the waste-basket and missed."

"But that means," Becky pulled her thoughts to-gether. "Mr. Ferrell wrote the note tied to the knife!"

"Yep!" Amy Jo nodded. "That's what's been at the back of my mind since we left the ice cream stand," she continued. "Remember, Paige said that she had written those flavors with a backward slant and she's left-handed. What was tucked away in the back of my mind was that I remember seeing Mr. Ferrell use his left hand to write at his desk."

Becky's eyes trailed to the desk. "Yes, I remember that too now that you mention it." Then, another thought occurred to her. "But Mr. Barney only found out about the fingerprints from the phone call a few minutes ago."

"I already thought of that," said Amy Jo. "Mr. Ferrell must have been listening in on the extension at his desk and decided to warn somebody. And I think I know who that somebody is."

"Who?!" Becky asked, leaning forward.

"There's only one person it could be," Amy Jo answered.

Suddenly, they heard the sound of someone running towards the office.

CHAPTER 11

Two Witnesses

The screen door swung open and banged shut. Click, thump, click, thump.

The girls paled as they looked at each other. Amy Jo lifted her finger to her lips. Becky nodded her head.

Crossing to the desk, the man picked up the telephone and dialed.

"We'll have to pack up and leave tonight, right away." It was Mr. Ferrell's voice. He listened for a moment, then he said, "Look, it's all over, just get your things together and we'll leave."

He replaced the receiver and began shuffling papers in the wastebasket, finally dumping its contents out on the floor. "Where is it?!" he said frantically.

Suddenly, the screen door opened and Zelda rushed in, wide-eyed and furious. "What do you mean we have to leave tonight?!" she gasped. "How did they find out about us?!"

Mr. Ferrell whirled around when she walked in. "Security found that can in the dumpster. You were *stupid* to put it there!"

"I didn't have enough time to get rid of it!" Zelda shouted.

The magazine slipped off Becky's lap and she gasped trying to catch it.

Mr. Ferrell and Zelda froze, then they stepped around the door. Amy Jo looked up and stammered. "We don't know anything about what you don't want us to know anything about."

Zelda glared at Mr. Ferrell. "This is just great! Now we have two witnesses!"

"Keep your mouth shut, Zelda!" Mr. Ferrell hissed. "They're just a couple of kids. They probably don't know anything."

Zelda snorted. "They've probably got everything figured out! They've been tailing us for the past three days!"

Zelda began pacing but stopped and turned to Mr. Ferrell. "Well, we can't just let them walk out of here," she said. "They'll tell Barney everything. We have to get rid of them."

"Well, what do you suggest we do with them?" he snorted. "Arrange a little *accident* here in my office?!"

Becky sucked in her breath and looked over at Amy Jo.

"Why don't you just let us go?" Amy Jo suggested. "We'll get our ponies and ride home. We won't tell anybody we saw you or *anything*."

"You're probably not even left-handed," Becky added, her voice squeaking.

Amy Jo closed her eyes and dropped her head.

"Just a couple of kids, huh!" Zelda said, her voice rising. She walked over to the window and looked out. "Barney could be back any minute."

"Barney went into town to talk to the police." Mr. Ferrell pressed his fist to his forehead.

"We can't just let them go," she said again, waving her arm wildly towards the girls. "Tie them up. We'll take them over to my trailer and figure something out there."

"No, we might run into somebody on the way," Mr. Ferrell said, rubbing his forehead again. "You go get the car and bring it around back. I'll figure something out while you're gone."

Zelda hesitated and looked at the girls.

"Hurry up!" Mr. Ferrell commanded.

Zelda studied him a few seconds, then she turned and walked out the door.

Mr. Ferrell began to pace the floor, his jaw muscles working, his lips set in a firm line.

Becky leaned close to Amy Jo and whispered. "Was Zelda the one you were thinking of?"

Amy Jo nodded.

"What made you think it was Zelda?"

"There wasn't any blood on her dress until she put her hand up to her shoulder," Amy Jo explained. "A cut like that should have bled right away. We saw her the next day and her shoulder was fine."

"She faked the whole thing?" Becky asked softly.

Amy Jo nodded again.

Mr. Ferrell stopped in front of the door and muttered. "It won't be easy, but it's the only thing we can do."

"What do you think he means?" Becky whispered nervously, looking at Amy Jo.

"I don't know," she answered, her eyes darting around the room. "Let's keep him talking; maybe Mr. Barney will come back."

Mr. Ferrell walked over to where the girls were sitting. "Everything might have worked if it hadn't been for the two of you." He placed his fist in his hand and twisted it.

"Well, ah," Amy Jo began, looking at his fist, "I think it's only fair to tell you that I have a black belt in karate."

"What are you talking about?" he frown.

"What I mean is," Amy Jo continued, "I wouldn't want to hurt you or anything, so if you just let us go, I promise not to chop you."

He raised his eyebrows and stared at her for a second. "Just sit there and keep your mouth shut!" he said, before strolling back to the door.

Amy Jo gave Becky a look that said, well, I tried. Becky closed her eyes and leaned her head against the wall.

Just then, they heard the sound of rain beating on top of a car as it pulled up to the front of the trailer. The steady rhythm of the windshield wipers kept time with the pulsating in their chests.

Becky grabbed Amy Jo's arm. "She's back! She scares me more than he does."

Amy Jo nodded and looked at the door to Mr. Barney's office, then glanced at Mr. Ferrell. *Maybe we could make a quick dash to the back door*, she thought desperately.

"I told her to come around the back!" he screeched, as he stormed out into the rain.

"Come on!" Amy Jo yanked Becky out of her chair and ran through Mr. Barney's office. She turned the handle to the back door and pushed. It was locked! Her

88

fingers fumbled around the door handle  looking for a way to turn a lever so that they could escape.

"Hurry!" Becky sobbed, looking over her shoulder.

Amy Jo gritted her teeth. "I'm trying!" Her fingers felt a lever and turned it. She shoved the door open and they pushed through it together.

The rain splattered their faces, making it difficult to see as they jumped off the back step. Arms reached out and grabbed them. Large, powerful hands were placed over their mouths. They kicked and struggled. It was agony to have nearly gotten away.

CHAPTER 12

Where the Action Is

"It's just a couple of kids," a voice hissed. "This one feels more like a wild cat."

"I thought I told you to go home." Mr. Barney's voice sounded both irritated and relieved.

The girls stared in the direction of the voice; rain plastered hair to their heads.

"It's Officer Higgins and his men," he continued. "They've been hiding here waiting for Zelda to get back before they move in."

"Now, if you promise to be quiet, my men will take their hands away," Officer Higgins said softly.

Two heads bobbed up and down and the powerful hands came away. The girls leaned up against the trailer, closing their eyes with relief while rain continued to drip down their cheeks.

"Okay, boys," Officer Higgins said. "Let's circle round to the front; we don't want them to get away."

Amy Jo turned her head and watched the police officers crouch down at the corner. "How'd you get here so fast?" she asked, turning back to Mr. Barney. "Mr. Ferrell said you left for town."

"That's what we wanted him to think," Mr. Barney answered, moving the girls under the shelter of the door's overhang. "We knew he had a partner, but we weren't sure who it was."

"Couldn't you tell by the fingerprints on the can?" she asked.

"There weren't any fingerprints," he answered. "We told him that, hoping he'd do something rash, and it worked."

"I don't get it," Becky said. "Why did you suspect Mr. Ferrell in the first place?"

"As soon as you girls showed me the note, I recognized Karl's handwriting. I also knew that he had to have a partner, an accomplice working with him inside the circus," Mr. Barney finished.

Amy Jo looked at him with disbelief. "Why didn't you tell us that you suspected Mr. Ferrell?"

"Well," Mr. Barney began, trying to skirt the truth without really lying, "you're the curious sort and I didn't want you to give the whole thing away or get into trouble." He scratched his head and thought for a second. "Looks like it didn't matter anyway," he finally decided.

The back door opened and an outside light switched on. "It's all clear in here now, Mr. Barney," Officer Higgins said, peering around the doorway.

"Right, thanks, Officer Higgins," Mr. Barney answered. He stepped through the door then motioned for the girls to follow him.

"You girls always seem to be where the action is," Officer Higgins commented as Amy Jo and Becky stood dripping in the middle of the floor. Then he shifted his attention to Mr. Barney. "Ferrell says Zelda's his sister, twin sister."

Mr. Barney's face registered shock. "Twin sister?" he asked. "Did they say anything else before your men took them to the police station?"

Officer Higgins shifted his weight a little, pulling his thoughts together. "Seems their father worked at this circus years ago, had Zorbon's job. Ferrell said he'd worked with his father since he was a young kid. He was to have followed in his father's footsteps when the older man retired."

Mr. Barney signaled for everyone to sit down.

The officer took a deep breath and continued. "Some money came up missing and their dad was accused. He lost his job and they had to leave. Zelda never got over it. She wanted to be her brother's assistant, not Zorbon's. Ferrell tried to scare Zorbon off or get him fired, but Zelda was out for revenge. She set out to wear away Zorbon's confidence . . . make him nervous during performances."

"She faked that knife accident," said Amy Jo with indignation. "That's the other thing that was in the back of my mind," she added, looking at her friend. "No blood showed until she reached up to touch her shoulder."

Mr. Barney looked at her with surprise. "I should have been more suspicious at the time. The doctor said there wasn't a mark on her when he checked her. She carried a little packet of fake blood and squeezed it on her shoulder herself, tried to tell the doctor it was some kind of stunt she and Zorbon had practiced to get a reaction from the audience."

Officer Higgins shook his head. "There's a lot we'll need to find out about those two."

"I know one thing!" Amy Jo chimed in. "They're both left-handed!"

"And they both disguised themselves as clowns," Becky added.

Officer Higgins raised his eyebrows. "How do you know that?"

"Zelda lit the match with her left hand when she started the fire," Amy Jo cut in. "Then we found a note Mr. Ferrell had written at his desk using his left hand and it matched the handwriting of the note we took off the knife," she finished, flushing a little as both men stared at her.

Mr. Barney studied Amy Jo with a twinkle in his eyes. "I suppose I should have put you girls on my security staff."

"Well," she answered, shrugging her shoulders, "we sort of like working by ourselves, right, Beck?"

Becky sighed. "Right now I'd just like to go home and get some dry clothes on."

"I think we can manage that," said Mr. Barney as all four rose from their chairs.

An officer was standing beside one of the police cars as Officer Higgins led the other three through the screen door.

Remembering Oreo and Ginger, Amy Jo asked, "What about our ponies? May they stay here tonight?"

"We can come back and get them tomorrow," Becky added.

"Sure," Mr. Barney said. "We'll take real good care of them for you."

Officer Higgins opened the back door of the car and helped the girls get settled. "I don't suppose you two will ever learn to stay out of trouble," he said with only half a smile. Then he closed the door tightly and signaled the driver to leave.

The girls sunk their exhausted heads against the back of the seat. Tense muscles began to relax.

"Glad this case is over," Amy Jo remarked, not bothering to cover a yawn.

"Me, too," Becky murmured, snuggling into her corner of the car.

Amy Jo rolled her head to the side and looked at Becky. "Maybe we could get a job mucking out stalls or something," she said sleepily. "That's pretty safe."

"Safe?" Becky answered with one eye open. "Nothing is ever safe when you're around."